A GOLDEN BOOK • NEW YORK

Copyright © 2000 by the Richard Scarry Corporation. All rights reserved. This 2014 edition was published in the United States by Golden Books, an imprint of Random House Children's Books, a division of Random House LLC, 1745 Broadway, New York, NY 10019, and in Canada by Random House of Canada Limited, Toronto, Penguin Random House Companies. Originally published in a slightly different form by Random House Children's Books, New York, in 2000. Published with the authorization of Les Livres du Dragon d'Or. Golden Books, A Golden Book, and the G colophon are registered trademarks of Random House LLC.
Visit us on the Web! randomhouse.com/kids
Educators and librarians, for a variety of teaching tools, visit us at RHTeachersLibrarians.com
Library of Congress Control Number: 2013032347
ISBN: 978-0-385-38804-7
MANUFACTURED IN MALAYSIA
10 9 8 7 6 5 4 3 2 1

Richard Scarry's

THE NIGHT BEFORE THE NIGHT BEFORE CHRISTMAS!

A GOLDEN BOOK • NEW YORK

'Twas the night before the night before the night before Christmas, and all through the Cat family house, not a creature was stirring . . . almost.

Sally Cat can't sleep.

"Huckle?" Sally asks. "When is Santa coming? I can't wait any longer for Christmas!"

"Just a few more days, Sally," Huckle says. "Now go back to sleep. Good night!"

Christmas Spirit

"Oh, my!" says Mr. Frumble. "It's almost Christmas!"

Mr. Frumble loves Christmas, because then he can help others in the true Christmas spirit.

He holds the door open at the grocery store. But that doesn't make Grocer Hank very happy.

Mr. Frumble offers to shovel snow. But that doesn't make Father Cat very happy.

Mr. Frumble offers to carry Hilda Hippo's Christmas gifts.
He helps Mr. Gronkle put his Christmas tree in his car.

But he makes no one happy.
"Hmm," says Mr. Frumble. "If no one
in Busytown needs my help before
Christmas, I think I know someone else
who does!"

Mr. Frumble gets into his pickle car and drives over to Mr. Fixit's workshop.

Does Mr. Fixit need Mr. Frumble's help?
Of course not!
Mr. Frumble needs Mr. Fixit's help!

Mr. Frumble explains to Mr. Fixit what he needs.
"No trouble at all, Mr. Frumble!" Mr. Fixit replies. "I can do that in a jiffy."
"Oh, thank you, Mr. Fixit," Mr. Frumble says.

A moment later, Mr. Fixit reappears, pushing Mr. Frumble's pickle car outside.
"*Voilà!*" he says proudly. . . .

"Your ski-pickle-doo!"

"Oh . . . my," gulps Mr. Frumble.

"And so that you can find your way, here is a compass to point you all the way to the North Pole," says Mr. Fixit.

"What are you going to do at the North Pole?" asks Mr. Fixit.

"I'm going to someone who needs my help," answers Mr. Frumble. "I'm going to be one of Santa's helpers!"

"*Bon voyage!*" calls Mr. Fixit. "Don't forget to be home for Christmas! It's the day after tomorrow!"

Sproing!
Sproing! Sproing!
Sproing!

11

Look out, everybody!
Here comes Mr. Frumble!

Hey!

Sproing!

Sproing!

Oops!

Sproing!

12

13

Mr. Frumble rides
through rain.

He rides through fog.

He rides through snow.

He rides over tall mountains.

He rides down steep slopes!

Mr. Frumble rides
until the ski-pickle-doo . . .

Umpf!

. . . can be ridden no more!

17

Santa's New Helper

"Dear me!" says Mr. Frumble. "Poor ski-pickle-doo will need some repairs if I'm ever going to get to the North Pole! Lucky for me, that looks like a garage up ahead! I'm sure they can help me!"

Mr. Frumble walks in the door. "Fill 'er up, please?" he calls. "Check the oil and water! Clean the windshield, please! . . . Um . . . is anybody here?"

Suddenly, Mr. Frumble slips on a puddle of water. *WHOA! BOOM!*

"Ho! Ho! Ho! And who are you?" asks a great big fellow in red trousers. Mr. Frumble explains that he needs his ski-pickle-doo repaired so that he can get to the North Pole.

"Ho, ho, but you ARE at the North Pole! I'm Santa Bear, and these are all my helpers.

"Welcome!

"I'm afraid we're too busy making toys for all the good girls and boys to repair your ski-pickle-doo today," says Santa Bear.

"Christmas is just two days away," says Santa Bear, pointing to the calendar on the wall.

"No . . . wait!" he cries. "Ho, ho . . . Oh, NO! It's already December 24! It's Christmas Eve!"

"Helpers!" shouts Santa Bear. "Hurry! I have to go!

"Get the sleigh ready and bring the presents!"

"But we haven't finished yet!" squeak his helpers.

"Good-bye, helpers!"
Santa Bear calls, climbing
the stairs to his sleigh.

Don't forget your hat, Santa Bear!

23

Santa Bear climbs into his big red sleigh.
"Are you ready, deers?" he asks.

He shakes the reins . . .

. . . and away he soars!

Mr. Frumble holds a calendar page in his hands. "Um . . . I think this came off when I came in," he says.

"Oh, no!" squeak the helpers. "Santa Bear has made a mistake! It isn't the night before Christmas . . . it's the night BEFORE the night before Christmas!"

25

The Night Before the Night Before Christmas

Santa Bear flies over Busytown.
"That's odd," Santa Bear says.
"There are no Christmas lights on this year!"

Santa Bear lands on the first rooftop and disappears down the chimney with his big bag of toys.

"*Humpf!*" says Santa Bear. "This family has forgotten to decorate its Christmas tree!"

27

Santa Bear continues to make his rounds through Busytown.

"This is a very strange Christmas," says Santa Bear. "Huckle, Sally, and Lowly haven't hung up their stockings on the fireplace!

"Hilda hasn't left a cup of cocoa and a plate of cookies, as she does every night before Christmas!

"Sergeant Murphy hasn't even unwrapped his Christmas tree!"

Finally, Santa Bear arrives at Mr. Frumble's house.
He slides with his bag down Mr. Frumble's chimney,
but Mr. Frumble has turned his fireplace into a
broom closet—and it's locked!
Santa Bear's sack has become stuck above him.

"Ho, ho," says Santa Bear. "What do I do now?"

Santa Frumble

"What do we do now?" asks Mr. Frumble. "We have to help Santa Bear!" say Santa Bear's helpers.

"Someone has to take Santa Bear's place and deliver the toys to all the good boys and girls for Christmas!" says one of Santa Bear's helpers.

"But who will take Santa Bear's place?" asks Mr. Frumble.

"YOU will!" answer all of Santa Bear's helpers.

"ME? Santa?"

Meanwhile, the good boys and girls of Busytown can't understand why they all received presents before Christmas Eve, and why all the boxes are empty!

"There must be a mistake!" says Lowly.

Santa Bear's helpers work busily all day to finish
the toys which they couldn't give to Santa Bear.
They also repair Mr. Frumble's ski-pickle-doo.

Mr. Frumble helps the
helpers fill the toy sack.

"How will we get to Busytown?" Mr. Frumble asks.

"We will pull you!" say Santa Bear's helpers.

"But we don't know where Busytown is!" says one of Santa Bear's helpers.

"Ah! But my hat does!" replies Mr. Frumble. "Hat always finds his way home!"

Mr. Frumble takes off his hat and tosses it in the air.

Off flies the hat.
Off fly Santa Frumble and his busy helpers!

Good luck, Santa Frumble!

Tonight is
the night before
Christmas!

All of Busytown
is decorated with
colorful Christmas
lights!

Santa Frumble lands at the Cat family house. *Swish!*

He climbs off his ski-pickle-doo.

"Um . . . who goes down the chimney?"
Santa Frumble asks the helpers.
"YOU do!" they all reply.

Santa Frumble climbs down the Cat family chimney.

BOOM!

Shhh, Santa Frumble! You don't want to wake the children!

Santa Frumble fills the stockings that Huckle, Sally, and Lowly have hung on the fireplace.

Then he sits down to sip some hot cocoa and eat the cookies the children have left for Santa Bear.

Santa Frumble gets up but trips in the dark. Whoops! There goes the tree! *CRASH!* Shhh, Santa Frumble!

"Did you hear that?" says Sally excitedly. "I'll bet that was Santa!"

"Shhh!" whispers Huckle. "Go back to sleep, Sally. . . . If Santa knows you're awake, he won't leave you a present."

Santa Frumble hurries on his way.

Santa Frumble visits Hilda Hippo's house.

He visits Sergeant Murphy's house.

And after he has visited every other house in Busytown, Santa Frumble arrives at his own house.

Santa Frumble
looks down his
chimney.

But Santa Frumble decides to enter his house through the front door.

What a clever Santa you are, Mr. Frumble!

He opens the broom closet.
"My hat!" he says.
"Our Santa!" say all of
Santa Bear's helpers.

41

"What are you doing here?"
Santa Bear asks Mr. Frumble.
    "There was a big mistake at
the North Pole," says Mr. Frumble.
    "You left on the night before
the night before Christmas!"
say Santa Bear's helpers.

Thank goodness Santa Frumble was there to bring all the presents to good boys and girls on the night before Christmas!

Santa Bear thanks Santa Frumble and rides back to the North Pole on his empty toy sack.

There is nothing left in the sack,
so Santa Bear leaves Mr. Frumble
the best present he can think of!

TO MY
NUMBER ONE HELPER,
MR. FRUMBLE!

MERRY CHRISTMAS!

SANTA BEAR

Wow! How about that!

Who Invented It
&
What Makes It Work?

By Sarah Leslie

Illustrated by Tom O'Sullivan

Who Invented It & What Makes It Work?

By Sarah Leslie

Illustrated by Tom O'Sullivan

Platt & Munk, Publishers/New York

A Division of Grosset & Dunlap

ISBN 0-448-47612-6 (Trade Edition)
ISBN 0-448-13037-8 (Library Edition)

Contents

The Balloon
The Montgolfier Brothers

Joseph and Jacques Montgolfier were the first to successfully conquer the air with their invention of the balloon. People had always wanted to fly, but until the Montgolfier brothers discovered that by filling a bag with hot air it floated, no one had been successful. Their first balloon, which was ten feet in circumference and made from linen lined with paper, was beautifully painted. It flew on June 5, 1783, carrying three passengers: a duck, a rooster, and a sheep. At the time, people thought that such a flght might be harmful, but all the passengers were found to be in excellent health when they reached the ground (except for the rooster, who was kicked by the sheep.)

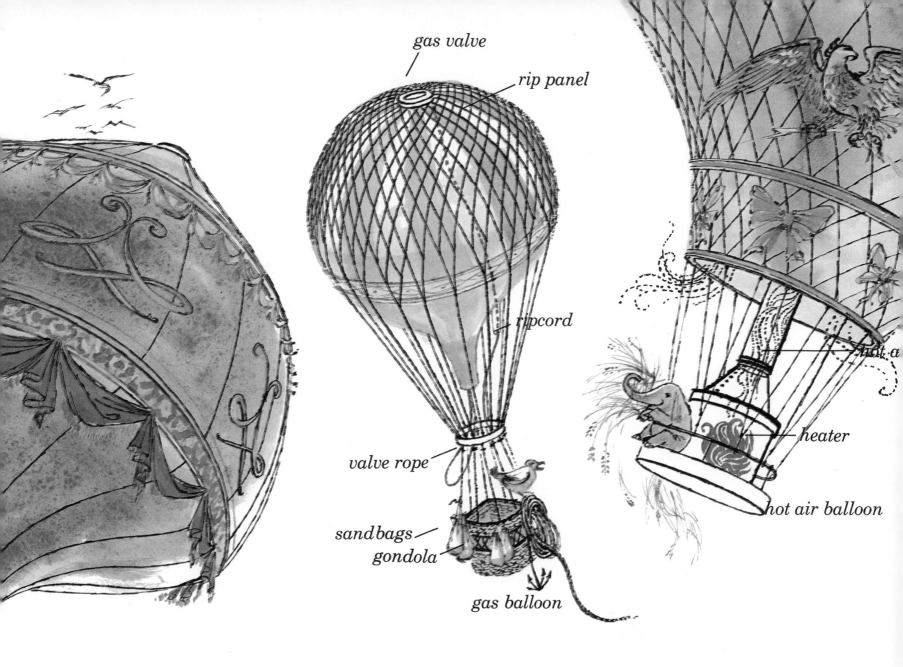

A balloon floats because it is a bag filled with a gas lighter than air. The first balloon was filled with hot air. The Montgolfier brothers discovered that hot air was lighter than cold air. They lit a large fire beneath their balloon, and up it went. Either a fire can be built on the ground, or, a heater can be hung beneath the balloon to keep the air hot. A later invention—the gas filled balloon—is filled with a gas which is lighter than air, such as helium. These balloons carry sandbags in the gondola. To lower the balloon, let out a bit of gas. To raise the balloon, throw off some sandbags.

The Clock
Christiaan Huygens

The principle of the clock was discovered by Galileo. When he was a young medical student, he noticed a lamp swinging in the cathedral at Pisa. He timed it by counting his pulse beats and realized that a pendulum could be used to measure time. But it wasn't until 1656 that Christiaan Huygens, a Dutch mathematician and physicist used this principle to build a pendulum clock. Before clocks were invented, people told time by using sundials or hour glasses. The sundial is a circle marked at intervals. As the sun casts its shadow on the centerpiece, the shadow moves around the dial. An hourglass is filled with a measured amount of sand. When all the sand has run from one side to the other, one knows that a certain amount of time has passed.

Clocks need power to run. Some run on electricity, some wind up, and some have pendulums. Pendulum clocks use a weight for power. As the weight slowly drops, it turns the gears. The pendulum gives it the proper timing for its drop. Wind up clocks use a tightly coiled spring for power. As the spring slowly unwinds, it turns lots of gears and moves the hands of the clock. The hairspring gives it the proper timing. Electric clocks use alternating electrical current. Since this kind of electricity has its own fixed timing, the electricity provides both the power and the timing.

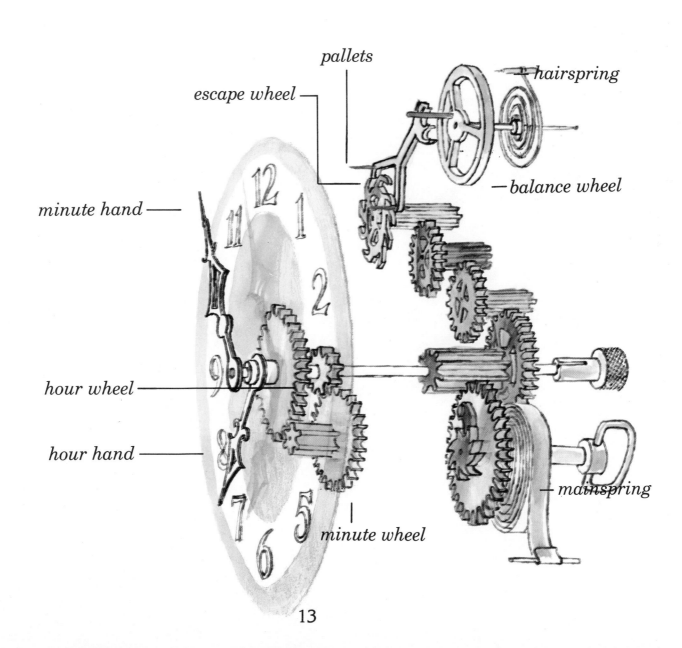

pallets

escape wheel

hairspring

balance wheel

minute hand

hour wheel

hour hand

mainspring

minute wheel

The Dynamo
Michael Faraday

Michael Faraday was an apprentice bookbinder. He started reading the books he was binding and became interested in science—especially in magnets and magnetism. In 1831 while working in his laboratory with a magnet and some iron filings, he discovered that the magnet could make the little pieces of iron move around. He called this "magnetic force". By putting a moving coil between the two ends of a horseshoe magnet he discovered that he could turn this magnetic force into electrical force or energy.

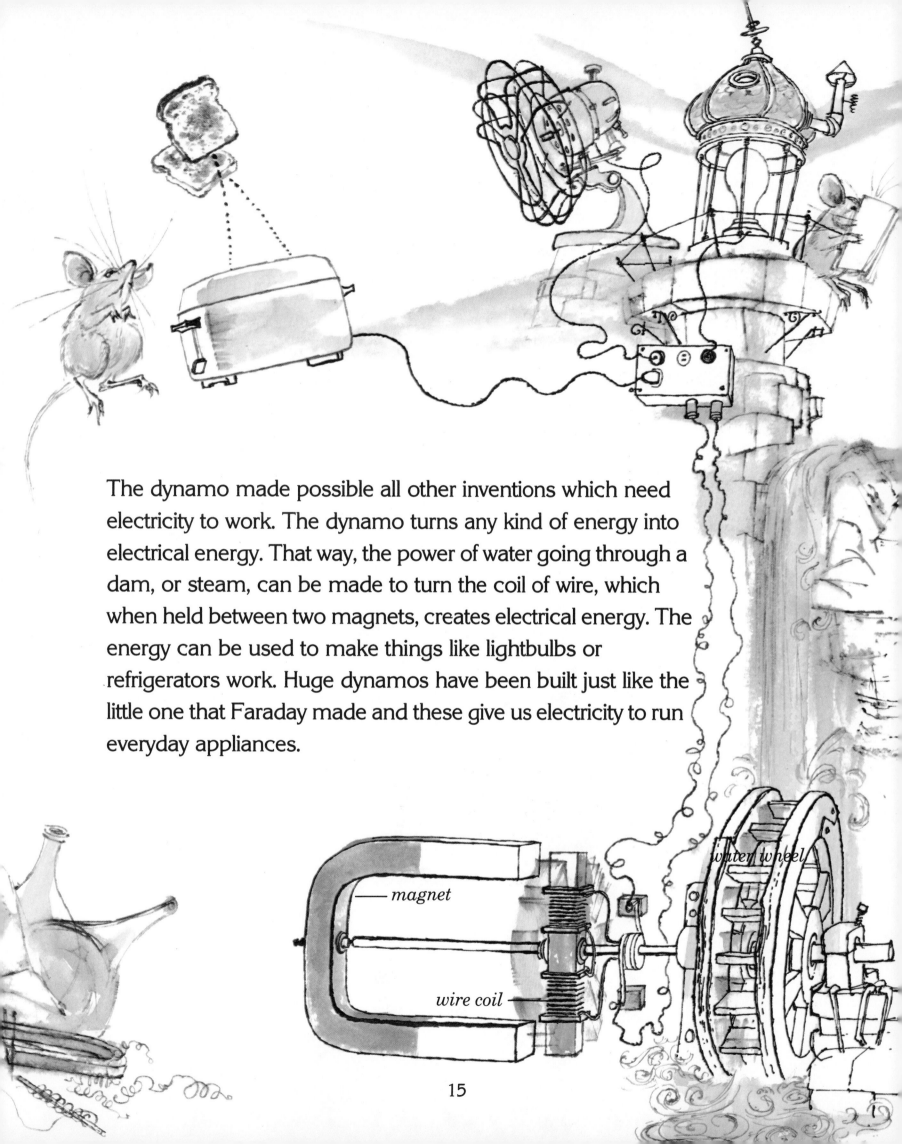

The dynamo made possible all other inventions which need electricity to work. The dynamo turns any kind of energy into electrical energy. That way, the power of water going through a dam, or steam, can be made to turn the coil of wire, which when held between two magnets, creates electrical energy. The energy can be used to make things like lightbulbs or refrigerators work. Huge dynamos have been built just like the little one that Faraday made and these give us electricity to run everyday appliances.

magnet

wire coil

water wheel

The Lightning Rod
Benjamin Franklin

Benjamin Franklin was interested in electricity. In 1752 people
didn't know much about the nature of electricity. Franklin
thought that lightning in the sky might very well be free
electricity in the atmosphere. One night during a big thunder
storm he went out with a kite. At the end of the kite string he
tied a metal key, and waited. Sure enough, lightning struck the
kite and Franklin got a shock from the key he held in his hand.
From all this he figured out that lightning was really electricity.

Benjamin Franklin had noticed that much damage was caused by lightning during big thunderstorms. He was looking for a way to keep the lightning from causing so much trouble. Since electricity tries to go into the ground, it first goes for the tallest thing around during a storm and travels through it to get to the earth. This might be a tree or a house. Sometimes when lightning hits, it sets whatever it hits on fire.

Franklin stuck a metal rod onto the roof of the house, or the church steeple. The lightning hit the rod and travelled all the way through it to the ground without setting fire to the house.

electrical current

17

The Piano
Bartolomeo Cristofori

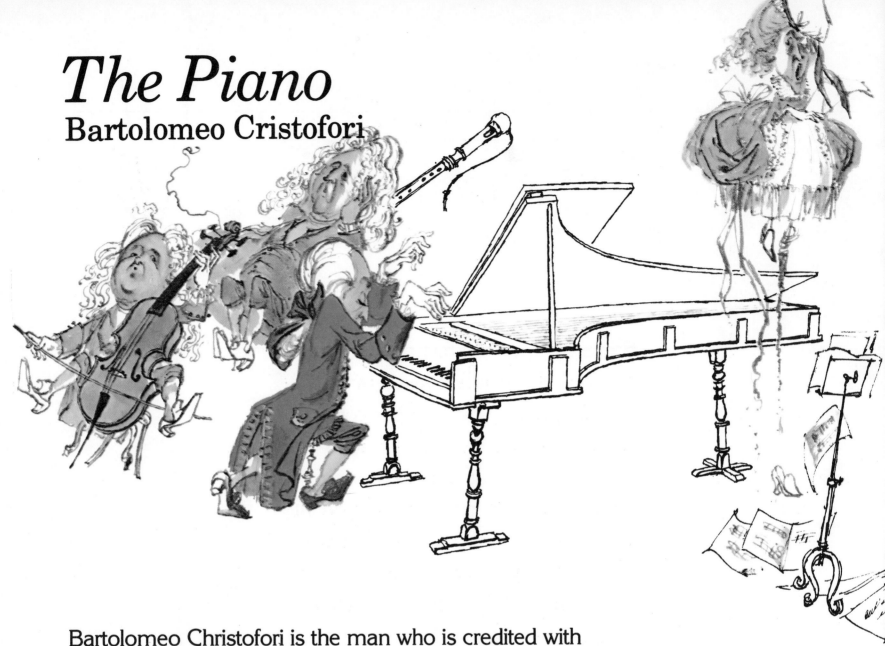

Bartolomeo Christofori is the man who is credited with inventing the first piano. Before the piano, there were musical instruments very much like it called the clavichord and the harpsichord. These instruments worked much the same way but they had no way of making the sound loud and soft. When you hit the key, no matter how hard you hit it, the sound was always the same. In 1709 Cristofori figured out a way to create loud and soft tones. Because the piano was so much more expressive than the harpsichord, it became far more popular as time went on. Soon, the piano became the most important solo instrument.

A piano is a large box with a row of keys outside, and a row of strings inside. The long strings are for the low notes, and the short strings are for the high notes. Each key on the keyboard is attached to a little hammer which, when pressed, hits one of the strings. Each string has a felt damper attached to the key bar. When the key is pressed and the hammer raised, the damper is also raised. This allows the string to vibrate. When the key is released, the damper comes back down on the string and stops the vibration and the sound. Underneath the row of strings is a sounding board which is a thin piece of wood. This also vibrates along with the string and makes the sound even louder.

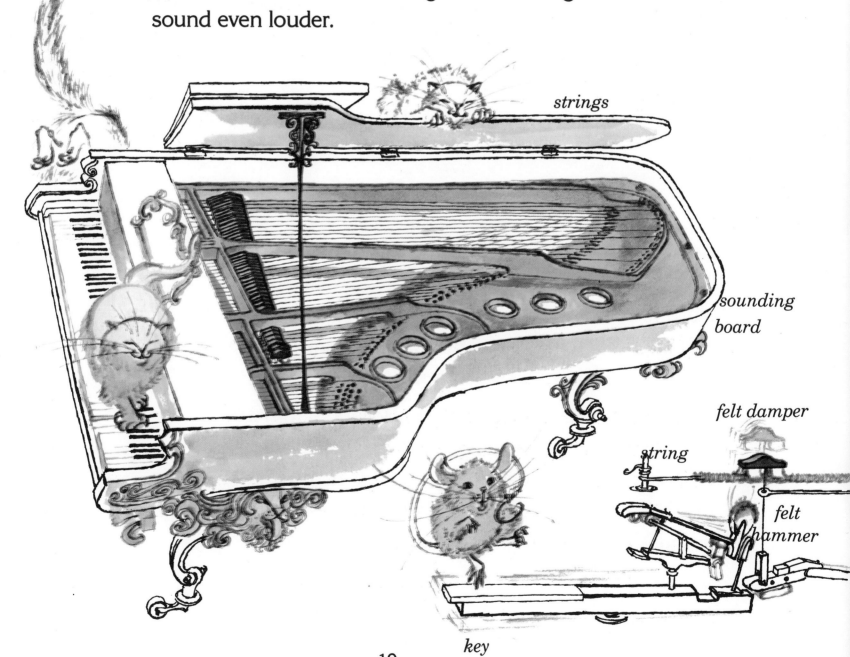

strings

sounding board

felt damper

string

felt hammer

key

The Telescope
Galileo Galilei

Galileo lived in Italy in the 16th century when people thought that the earth was in the center of the universe. (It isn't, but they didn't know that then.) Since he spent so much time looking up into the sky at things so far away, he thought it would be nice if he could see them a little better.

Learning that Hans Lippershey in Holland had made an instrument that made things far away look bigger and closer, Galileo decided to make one, too. First he made one that magnified things three times bigger and then he made one that magnified things thirty times bigger.

The kind of telescope that Galileo invented was called a "refracting" telescope. It uses two glass lenses like the kind in eyeglasses. The one in front is convex or thick and produces an image of what you are looking at on the second lens. The second lens is concave or thin in the middle, and makes that image bigger, though upside down. By making this second lens thin in the middle on both sides, like an apple core, the image gets turned right side up.

When Galileo looked through his telescope, he saw that the moon had mountains on it, that the planet Jupiter had four moons, and that there were rings around Saturn. No one had ever seen these things before.

convex lens   *concave lens*

The Airplane
Orville and Wilbur Wright

One of the most interesting events of the twentieth century happened at Kitty Hawk, North Carolina, on December 17, 1903. Orville and Wilbur Wright flew in a flying machine for the first time. Only a few newspapers carried a story about it at the time—the others didn't believe that it really had happened. Orville and Wilbur owned a bicycle shop, and had always been interested in flight. They practiced building gliders until they understood all the principles of flight, and then they tried to find a gasoline engine for their plane. They finally had to build one. The longest flight they made that day was 852 feet.

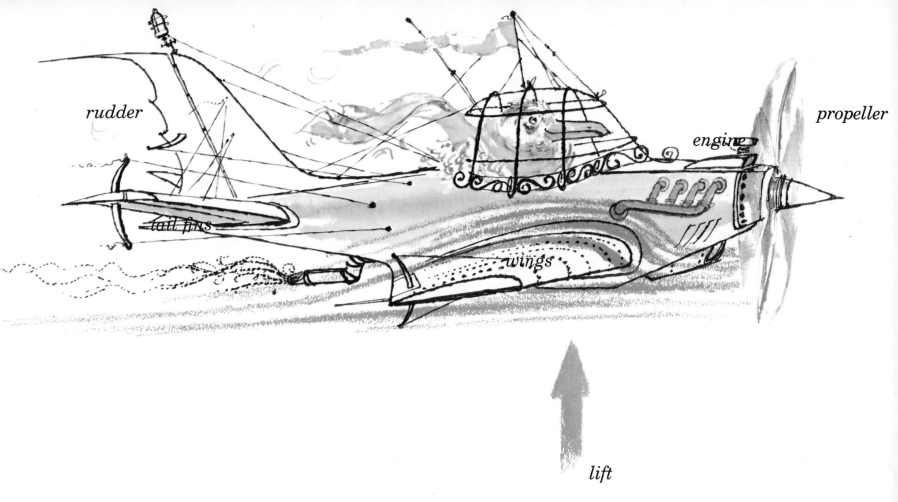

rudder

propeller

engine

tail fins

wings

lift

There are several important parts to an airplane: the wings, the propeller, the engine, the tail fins. The wings are shaped curved on the top, and flat on the bottom. When the engine turns the propeller, the blades of the propeller push the air back over the wings making the plane go forward. At the same time, the air rushing over the top curve of the wing moves faster than the air moving under the wings. This makes the air underneath push up strongly and makes the plane rise. The tail fins and rudder can be turned to stabilize the plane and make it go in different directions. The bigger the wings, the more weight they can lift with them up into the sky.

The Camera
Louis Daguerre

In the 18th century, a Swedish chemist discovered that certain types of silver were sensitive to light. In 1839, a Frenchman named Louis Daguerre made the first photographs. He first constructed a box with a hole in it that let light inside. After coating a piece of copper with silver iodide, he slipped it into the box and exposed it to the light. In the early days of the camera, people who wanted their picture taken had to sit still for a very long time in order for the light to react on the chemicals. Now, the film has been perfected so that only a second or two is needed to expose the film.

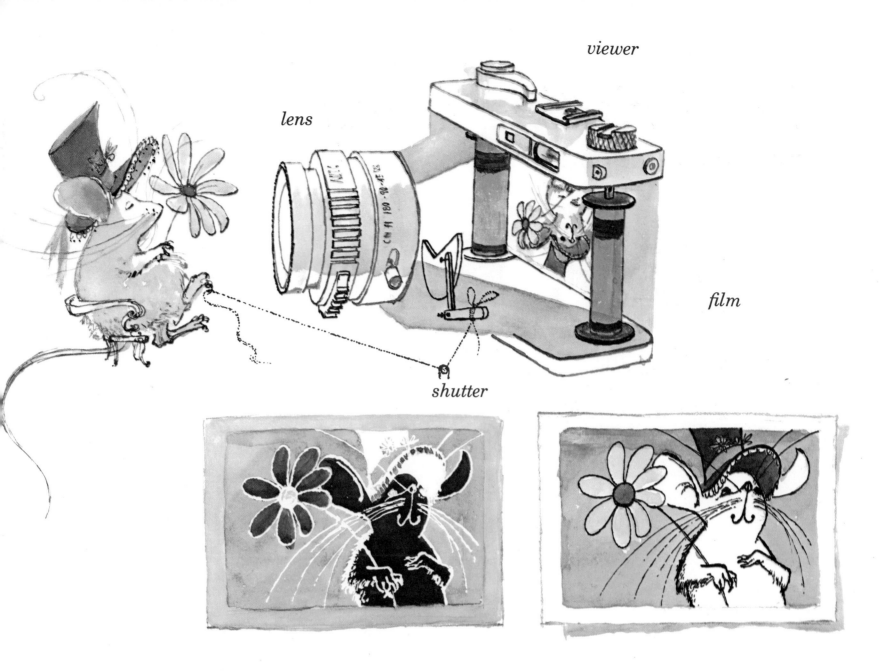

viewer

lens

film

shutter

The camera is a completely sealed box that lets the light which is reflected from an object be focused on a piece of light-sensitive film. A glass lens focuses the image and the shutter is a little door over a hole which opens and lets the light inside the box. The light-sensitive chemicals react according to the amount of light shown on them. When the film is placed in a special solution, the areas of the film that got the most light appear dark, and those that got the least light appear white. This is the negative, and when it is processed, it produces a positive photograph.

The Printing Press
Johann Gutenberg

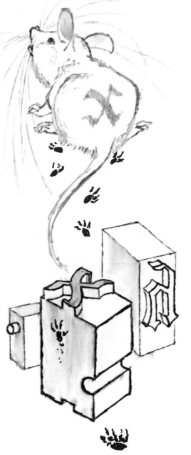

Before Johann Gutenberg invented the printing press, books were made by scribes who copied the words by hand. It could take a whole year to make one book, so not too many people had books to read. Gutenberg thought everybody should have books, so he invented movable type. Movable type consists of metal castings of each letter of the alphabet. These are held together with wood frames. As his press, he used an old wine press. The first book that Gutenberg printed was the Bible, which he finished in 1440. After that, as more and more presses were built, more and more people were able to buy books and newspapers to read.

The type of press that Gutenberg invented used little blocks of metal that had raised letters. All these letters were arranged into words and sentences, in a frame. Then they were inked and the paper was pressed on the inked letters. That way a whole page, or two, could be printed at a time.

Now a press has large rollers. Instead of a flat frame for each page, there is a metal plate which can be wrapped around the rollers. As the paper slides under the rollers, the inked letters press down and make their impression on the page.

metal plate

metal plate

rollers

Bifocals
Benjamin Franklin

Benjamin Franklin didn't invent eyeglasses but he made a definite improvement on them. Eyeglasses are thought to have been invented in the 16th century in Italy by a man named Salvino Armati. By using a curved lens, held in front of the eye, people can see better. Some people can't see things far away, and some people can't see things up close. There is a different kind of curved lens for each person's problem. Some people, however, can't see well either far away or up close. They had to have two pairs of glasses. Franklin invented a single lens that had both kinds in one. He called them bifocals.

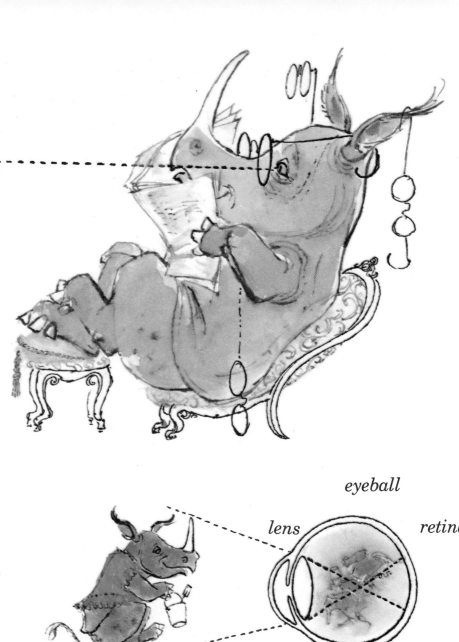

The eye is a round ball. When you look at something, the image of what you are looking at is projected on the back of the eyeball. This is called the retina. Sometimes, the eyeball is not a perfect circle, though. That means that the image isn't projected on the retina, only close to it. The optic nerve therefore cannot send a clear message to the brain. The lens in front of the eyeball helps move the image so that it will be sent right on to the retina. A convex lens which is curved out, or a concave lens which is curved in, is used. Bifocals have the top half of the lens concave and the bottom half convex. You look through the top to see far away and through the bottom to see close up.

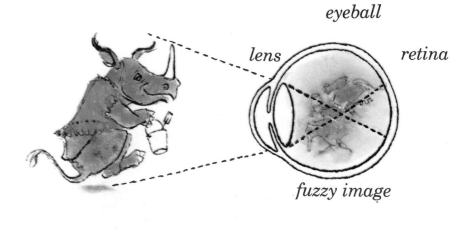

eyeball

lens   *retina*

fuzzy image

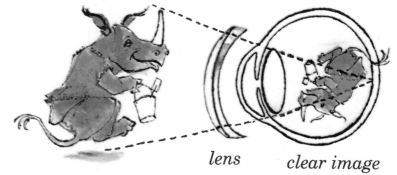

lens   *clear image*

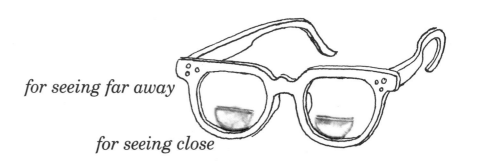

for seeing far away

for seeing close

The Electric Light Bulb
Thomas A. Edison

Thomas Edison was so busy inventing things that he was always losing jobs. However he invented some of the most important things we use today. When he was twelve years old he went to work for a railway as a train-boy. He sold more newspapers, books and fruit than any other boy. But he set up a laboratory in the back of one of the baggage cars so he could work on inventions, and one day, his chemicals were knocked over and set fire to the car. He was fired. One of Edison's most important inventions was the electric light bulb. Before that, light was produced by oil or gas lamps which were expensive and very dangerous.

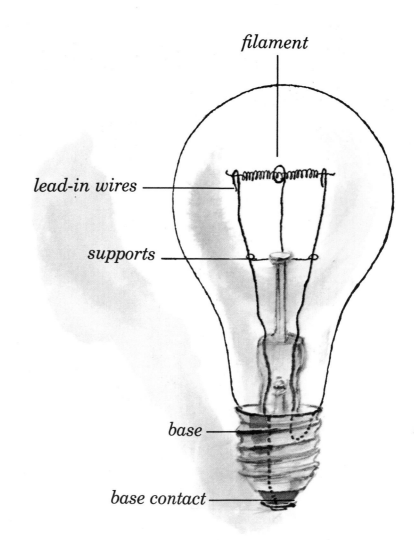

filament

lead-in wires

supports

base

base contact

The invention of the electric light bulb has made our lives very different. We can light streets, rooms, bridges or anything, safely and inexpensively. An electric light bulb is made out of a glass bulb with a very thin wire inside called a filament. The filament is made out of a metal which can get very hot and not melt. This is usually tungsten. When an electric current is passed through the filament, it glows white hot. In order that the filament not burn away, the air is removed from the bulb and is replaced sometimes by a gas which is inert such as argon or nitrogen.

The Phonograph
Thomas A. Edison

Edison learned to be a telegraph operator, and at fifteen he
was put in charge of an office. While at this job he made an
alarm clock to wake him up in time to send hourly dispatches.
He also invented a special machine that would repeat telegraph
messages that came in too fast for him to record. The repeater
simply relayed the message automatically to a second line
which ticked it off at a slower rate. When his boss learned of this
device, he was fired. However it gave him the idea for the
phonograph. He wrapped a sheet of tinfoil around a drum.
Turning the handle by hand he shouted a verse of "Mary Had A
Little Lamb" into the speaker. With an adjustment he turned the
handle again and out came his words. The public called him
"The Wizard of Menlo Park".

The phonograph reproduces the sounds recorded in the grooves of a record. A flat plate (the turntable) is connected to an electric motor which makes it go around. There is a pickup arm which has a cartridge and a stylus or needle on it. When the needle is placed on the record, it vibrates in the fine wiggily spiral groove and these vibrations are transferred to a special crystal in the cartridge. When squeezed, bent, or twisted, this crystal produces tiny electrical impulses that travel through a fine wire to the amplifier. The amplifier magnifies the impulses many times and the speaker turns them into sound.

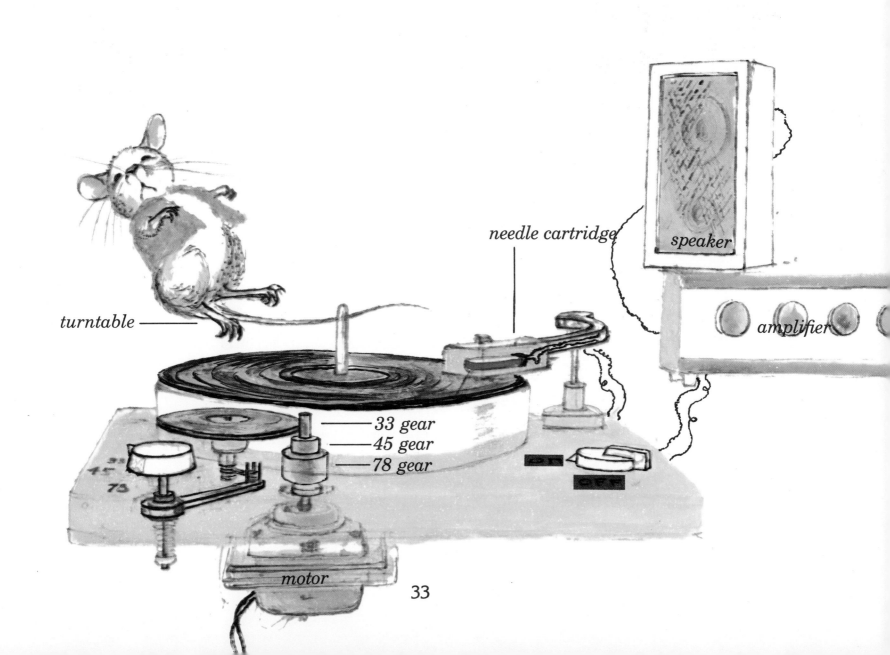

needle cartridge

speaker

turntable

amplifier

33 gear
45 gear
78 gear

motor

Motion Pictures
Thomas A. Edison

Edison decided that he should invent something that would do for the eye what the phonograph had done for the ear. He worked for two years and in 1889 made the "kinetograph" which was the first motion picture camera. It took many pictures in a very short period of time so that every part of an action was shown. Then he invented the "kinetoscope" which was the forerunner of the projector. This showed the pictures in quick succession so they looked like one smooth movement instead of lots of pictures in a row. In 1912 he invented the "kinetophone" which linked the film camera with the phonograph and made a talking picture.

After the movie camera takes the many, many pictures, the long roll of film is put into the projector. Inside the projector is a light bulb. Behind the bulb is a mirror that makes sure that all the light is shown forward through a special lens which spreads the light evenly over the film. The rays go through the film and shine it onto the screen. On the sides of the film are little holes. A little sprocket wheel goes into the holes, and as the wheel turns, the film is moved quickly past the lens. The film also has a strip along the edge which is coated with iron oxide particles. This is where the sound is recorded.

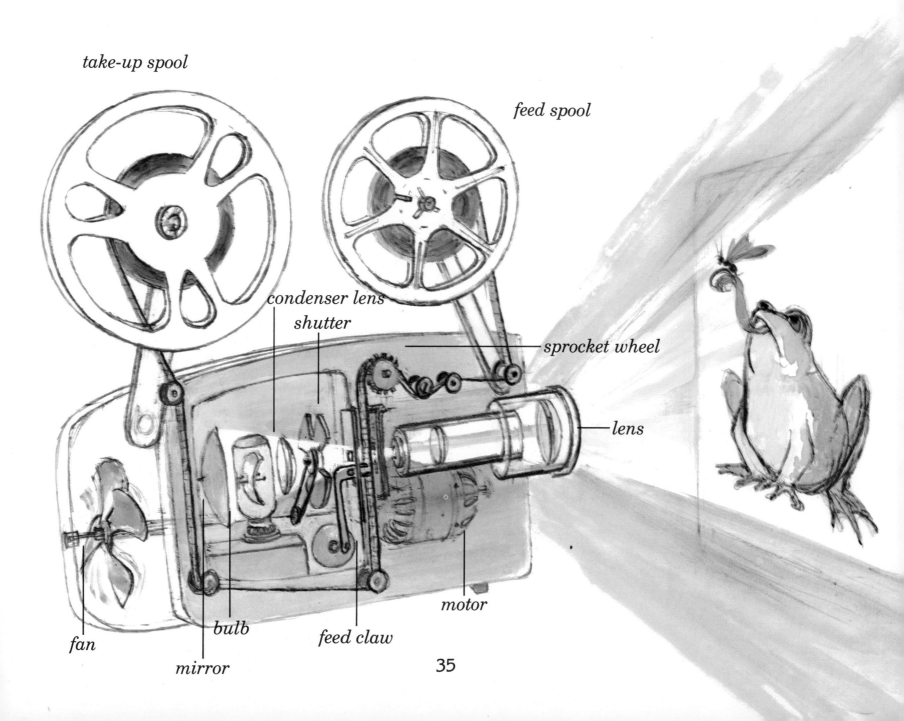

take-up spool

feed spool

condenser lens

shutter

sprocket wheel

lens

motor

fan

bulb

feed claw

mirror

35

Animated Cartoon Movies
Winsor McCay

Winsor McCay was the man who invented the special way of doing drawings for animation in motion pictures. Instead of taking many pictures of an action the way Edison did for motion pictures, he drew many drawings that served the same purpose. He was a cartoonist who had a cartoon strip character called "Little Nemo" in the newspaper. He made his first animated cartoon film of "Little Nemo" in 1910. Then came "Gertie the Dinosaur" and others. Before that there were a few toys that made animated cartoons. The first was called a Thaumatrope, made in 1826. There was also the Praxinoscope and the flitter pad.

Animated cartoons work in the same way that motion pictures do. Many pictures, each showing a small segment of walking for example, when shown in quick succession, make the viewers think they have seen one smooth movement. The Thaumatrope, the first cartoon toy, was a cardboard disc that had a picture on either side. When the string that held it was flipped quickly, the two pictures seemed to combine into one. The Praxinoscope was a large cardboard disc with pictures on it. When it turned, the reflection of the pictures in mirrors made them seem to dance. The flitter pad is a book of drawings with slight changes in each page. When the pages are flipped the pictures seem to combine and move.

Thaumatrope

flitter pad

Praxinoscope

37

The Telegraph
Samuel Morse

The electric telegraph was the first long distance, rapid communication system ever developed. The man with the idea was Samuel Morse, a portrait painter. He got the idea on board a ship returning from England in 1832. In 1844, the first message was sent using his invention, between Baltimore and Washington.

The telegraph was made of a key switch and an electromagnet at each end in series with a wire and a battery. The earth acted as the return line. He also invented a special alphabet called the Morse Code, which is still used.

A telegraph system has a key and a sounder at each end of a wire. There is an electric battery to give it power to work. When the key is pressed down it sends an electrical pulse down the wire which energizes the sounder at the other end of the wire.

The code is a system of long and short pulses—dashes and dots—for each letter of the alphabet and numbers 0 to 9. Cables, which are lots of wires held together, have been laid under the ground or on poles all across the country and under the ocean, too. Now people can send telegrams almost anywhere in the world.

The Typewriter
Christopher Sholes

Before the invention of the typewriter, everything was written out by hand. Christopher Sholes was working on a machine that blind people could use to write with. He thought if he made a machine with all the letters of the alphabet in special places, that people who couldn't see would be able to write clearly. In 1843 he finally perfected his writing machine and called it a "chirographer". By 1873, people realized that it would be a great machine for everyone to use. It went into use in offices everywhere.

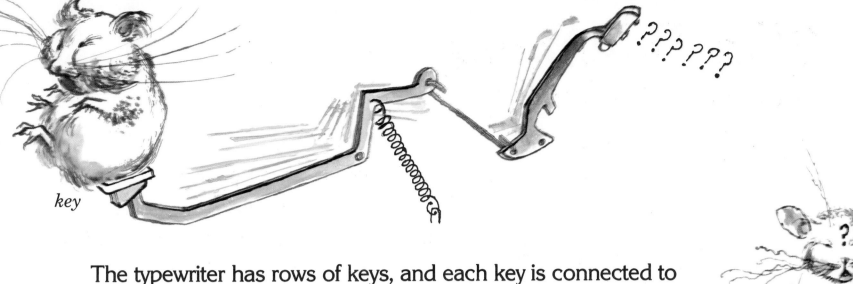

key

The typewriter has rows of keys, and each key is connected to a metal bar. The tip of the metal bar has a letter, symbol, or number on it which is the same as the one shown on the key. This metal letter is raised, and when the key is hit, the metal bar with the letter hits the inked ribbon, and presses it against the paper, making a letter. The carriage, along with the roller which the paper goes over, moves over one notch every time a key is hit. This is so the letters don't print one on top of another. All typewriters have the same arrangement of letters. If you learn where all the letters are on one typewriter, you will know them on all typewriters.

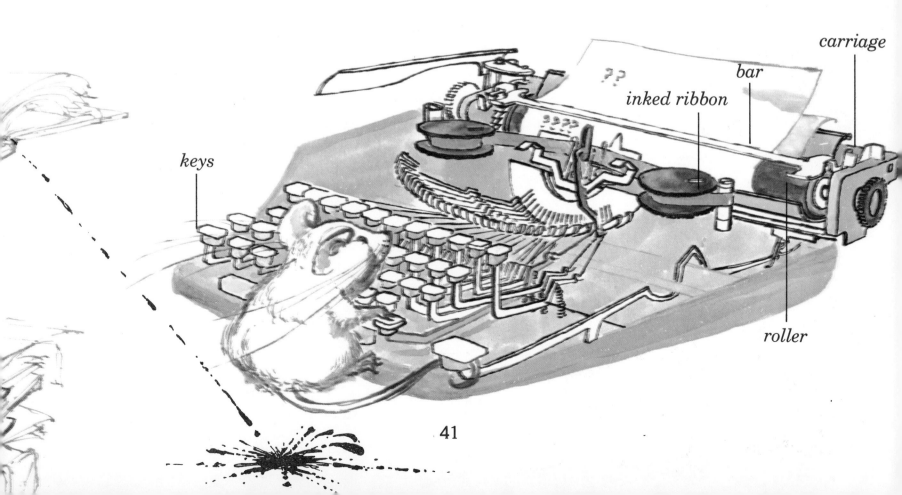

keys

inked ribbon

bar

carriage

roller

The Telephone
Alexander Graham Bell

Alexander Graham Bell invented the telephone because he was in love. It happened that Alexander's father and grandfather had devoted their lives to teaching the deaf and dumb to speak. This was also Alexander's profession. He fell in love with one of his pupils, Mabel Hubbard, and while trying to invent a device to improve her hearing, he discovered the principle that led to his invention of the telephone. After years of experimenting with ways to send speech over wires, he finally succeeded on March 10, 1876. On that day, his assistant, Thomas Watson, heard the first telephone message. It was "Mr. Watson, come here, I want you".

metal diaphragm

electromagnet

When someone speaks into the transmitter part of the telephone, sound waves hit a carbon diaphragm behind the mouthpiece. It vibrates and hits loosely packed carbon granules which are between the diaphragm and a plate behind it. The moving carbon grains change the amount of electricity passing along the wire connecting the two phones. The electrical impulses travel to the listener's receiver where they activate a small electromagnet. This causes a thin metal disc to vibrate. The metal disc vibrations produce the sounds we then hear from the receiver.

carbon granules

diaphragm

The Elevator
Elisha G. Otis

Elevators are what made possible the use of skyscrapers. During the Middle Ages there were very simple elevators used in monasteries to bring up people and supplies, but these were operated by hand. They were built with a rope and a pulley. In 1850 Henry Waterman made a crude hoist for heavy supplies. Elisha G. Otis invented a safety device which would keep the elevator car from falling if the ropes broke, and this made possible the passenger elevators we have today. His company invented the first electric elevator in 1889, and it's a good thing, too. Who would want to climb to the 95th floor everyday to go to work!

The elevator is a box in a shaft. The box is pulled up and down by an electric motor which winds a cable around a pulley. The box runs up and down in the shaft on guide rails which keep it straight. When passengers push the button for the floor they want, the electric motor automatically shuts off when the box reaches the floor. Then the elevator stops. A heavy weight is attached to the other end of the cable which balances the weight of the box. This way, the motor has to lift only the weight of the passengers. On either side of the shaft are big clamps. Should anything go wrong, if a cable should break, these clamps quickly grab the box and keep it from falling.

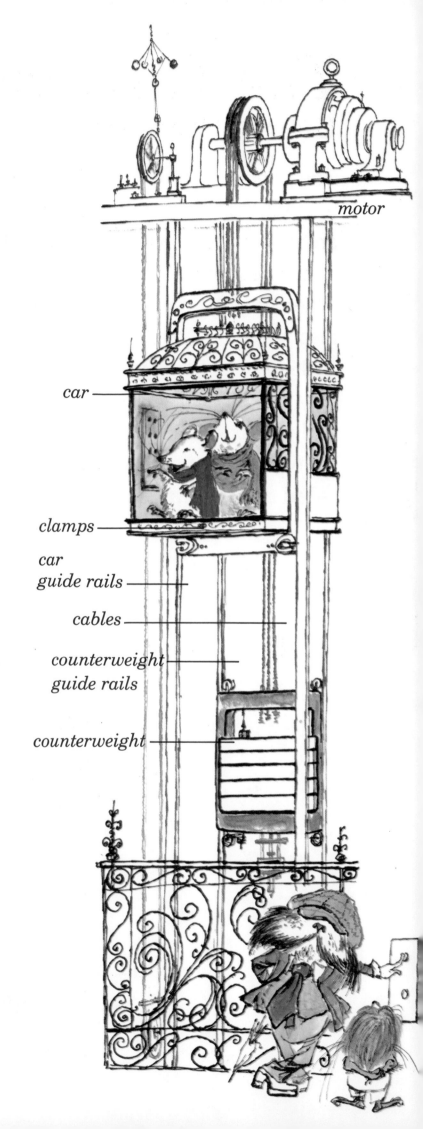

motor

car

clamps

car
guide rails

cables

counterweight
guide rails

counterweight

45

The Thermometer
Gabriel Fahrenheit

The principle of the thermometer was discovered by Galileo in 1593. But it wasn't the kind of thermometer we use when we are sick. It was an air thermometer, based on the idea that when things get hotter, they get bigger and take up more space. When they get colder, they shrink. Gabriel Fahrenheit discovered that mercury, which is a metal that has such a low melting point that it is usually found as a liquid, would make a very good thermometer. He placed mercury in a bulb at the end of a long thin tube that was marked off at regular intervals—degrees. The intervals that he came up with are now called degrees Fahrenheit.

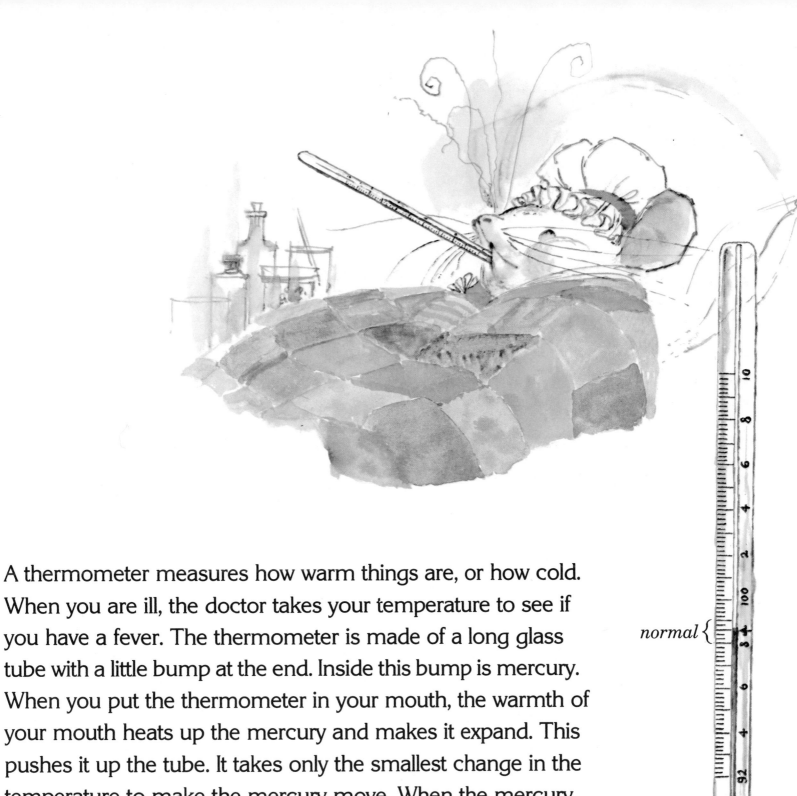

normal {

tube —

bulb with mercury —

A thermometer measures how warm things are, or how cold. When you are ill, the doctor takes your temperature to see if you have a fever. The thermometer is made of a long glass tube with a little bump at the end. Inside this bump is mercury. When you put the thermometer in your mouth, the warmth of your mouth heats up the mercury and makes it expand. This pushes it up the tube. It takes only the smallest change in the temperature to make the mercury move. When the mercury stops moving, you look at the numbers on the side of the tube to see what your temperature is. Normal for everyone is 98.6 degrees. If your temperature is higher, then you have a fever.

The Motorcycle
Gottlieb Daimler

Even though Americans made the car what it is today, they did
not invent it. The first steam car was made in 1770 in France.
The invention that made the car possible was the gasoline
engine, which is still used in cars. Gottlieb Daimler worked on
the production of the gasoline engine and, in 1885, used a
gasoline engine to power a bicycle. This was the first
motorcycle. Later, he built the Mercedes, a car which is still
being made and sold today. Shortly after Daimler's work, Henry
Ford in America began making his cars on the assembly line,
which made them much cheaper to buy.

A motorcycle works much the way a bicycle does, but instead of moving by leg power, it moves by a gasoline engine. The engine moves the back wheel with a chain, or a drive shaft. The handles on the front wheel steer the motorcycle, and the right handle grip is the "throttle" which controls the flow of gas, and thus the speed. There are two sets of brakes. Hand brakes on the handlebars for the front wheel, and a foot brake for the rear wheel.

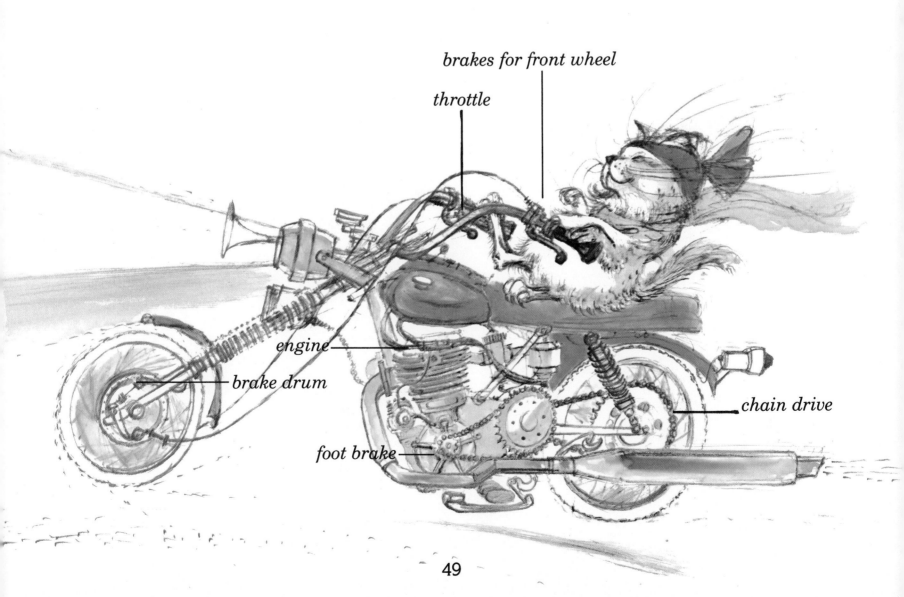

brakes for front wheel

throttle

engine

brake drum

chain drive

foot brake

The Zipper
Whitcomb Judson and Gideon Sundback

Whitcomb Judson invented the zipper. In 1891, he came up with the idea of a row of hooks and eyes which could be pulled together with a slide handle. He designed them to go on shoes, but thought they might work on almost anything. For a while, people put them on ladies' underwear, but they weren't really popular. Every time the ladies sat down, the hooks and eyes unhooked. Finally, Gideon Sundback discovered that interlocking metal teeth held together much better than the hooks and eyes. He patented his invention and soon there were zippers on almost everything.

The zipper is made of two long rows of metal notches, or teeth. The teeth are arranged so that each tooth faces the space between the two teeth on the opposite row. The little teeth are each shaped with a bump on the end and indents that are just the same shape at the bottom. When the little metal case with the pull handle on it slides over the two rows, it pulls them close together. As each tooth slides into the case, it slips into the space opposite. When the teeth are meshed in, they cannot be pulled apart because they fit so neatly together. When the little case is pulled down, the little teeth unmesh.

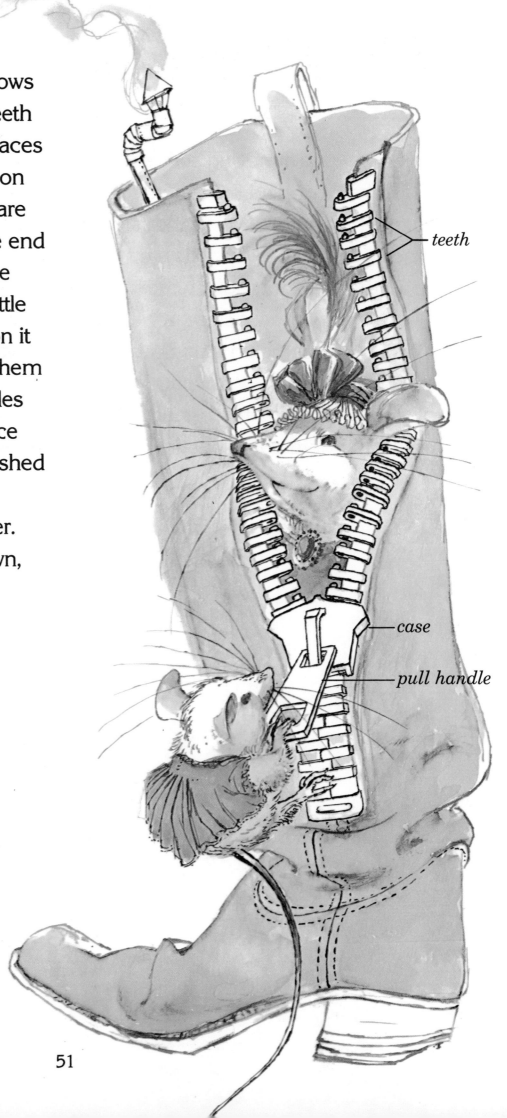

teeth

case

pull handle

51

The Escalator
Charles D. Seeberger

An escalator is a moving staircase. In fact that was what Charles D. Seeberger called it when he invented it. It was shown at the Paris exhibition of 1900 as the staircase of the future—which is exactly what it was. The Otis brothers, inventors of the elevator, saw it there, and manufactured it. The first escalator was put in Gimbels department store in New York where it stayed until 1938. At the same time as Seeberger was inventing his escalator, Mr. Reno was working on a similar stairway that had a platform with teeth in it instead of being flat. These two kinds of escalators were combined in 1921, and that is the only kind made today.

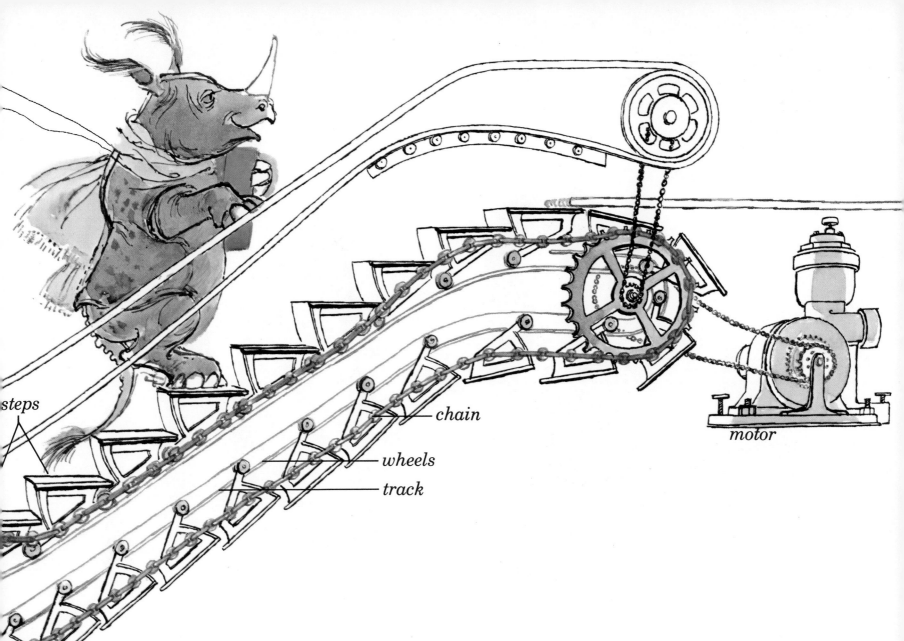

steps

chain

wheels

track

motor

An escalator is a row of steps pulled up a hill by a chain. The chain is pulled by a motor which is under the staircase. Each step is on little wheels that run up a track. At the top of the stairs, the steps flatten out by sliding on the track lower and lower until they seem to disappear under the floor. What actually happens is that the chain is continuing around under the staircase, carrying the steps along with it. Each step is like a little flatbed truck and carries one person all the way up.

Matches
John Walker

tinderbox

Before matches were invented, fire was made in several different ways. Indians made fire by rubbing sticks that were very dry in a small pile of wood shavings. After a long time, the sticks would get so hot from being rubbed that they would set fire to the wood shavings. In colonial times, people used flint and a piece of steel. They could "strike" sparks into a tinderbox of old rags to start a fire. In 1827 John Walker, a druggist, invented matches. These were splinters of wood dipped in a chemical mixture that got very hot when rubbed on sandpaper. They were called Lucifers.

The phosphorous mixture that was put on the tips of matches was so easy to light that sometimes people could light them by scraping the match on the bottoms of their shoes. But this was also somewhat dangerous. Sometimes, because it was so easy to set fire to phosphorous, the matches would simply light all by themselves if they were dropped. In 1911, Mr. W.A. Fairburn discovered a kind of phosphorous that wasn't so easy to light. Now, matches are made of wood, or paper, and the paper ones are kept in little cardboard "books".

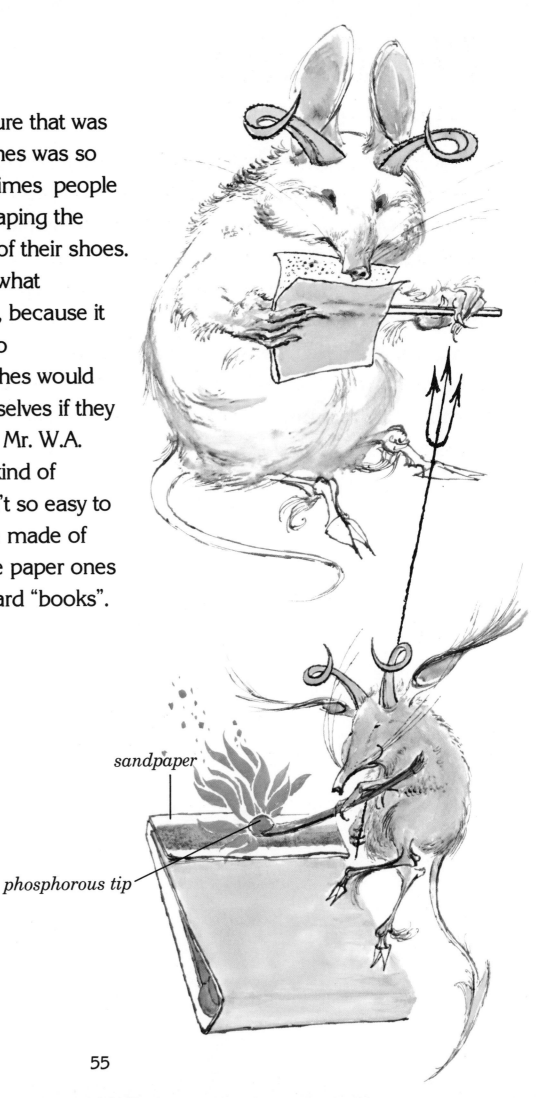

sandpaper

phosphorous tip

The Radio
Guglielmo Marconi

Guglielmo Marconi, an Italian inventor, developed radio telegraphy as we know it today. His invention was based on much previous work done in the field. He transmitted long wave signals in 1895 and sent signals over the ocean in 1901. His invention was based on the radio tube developed by Lee De Forest. De Forest was looking for a better way to make the telegraph work. He wanted it to work without wires. His radio tube made voice transmission possible. Marconi put together the tube and the tuner invented by Michael Pupin—and made a radio.

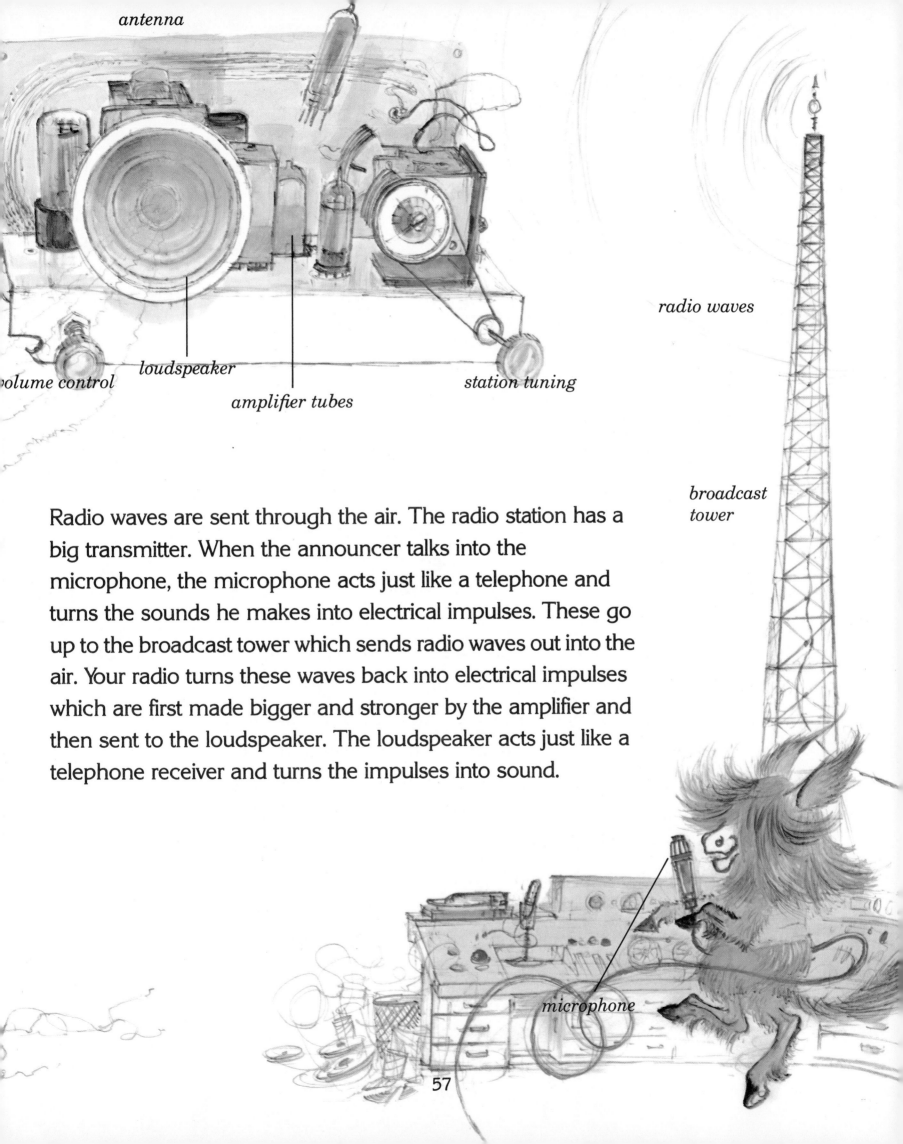

antenna

radio waves

broadcast tower

loudspeaker

volume control

amplifier tubes

station tuning

Radio waves are sent through the air. The radio station has a big transmitter. When the announcer talks into the microphone, the microphone acts just like a telephone and turns the sounds he makes into electrical impulses. These go up to the broadcast tower which sends radio waves out into the air. Your radio turns these waves back into electrical impulses which are first made bigger and stronger by the amplifier and then sent to the loudspeaker. The loudspeaker acts just like a telephone receiver and turns the impulses into sound.

microphone

The Refrigerator
Dr. John Gorrie

The first machine to manufacture ice in the United States was made by Dr. John Gorrie. Dr. Gorrie practiced in Florida which was, in 1839, trying to become a state. But people who wanted to live in Florida were few and far between because of the fear of malaria. Dr. Gorrie thought that this disease might be caused by the hot swamp vapors. His patients cried for ice and there was never enough. Dr. Gorrie worked on a machine that would cool water and turn it into ice. Finally, in 1850, he succeeded. Even though this was not the cure for malaria, which is caused by mosquito bites, it did help improve public health and sanitary conditions everywhere.

The workings of an ice making machine—or a refrigerator—are based on two important laws of physics. First, heat moves away from hot objects toward cool ones, and second, heat is needed when a liquid turns into a gas. An electric motor in the refrigerator powers a compressor which turns the freon gas into a liquid. This liquid then moves through tubes in the box where it changes back into a gas because it is no longer under pressure. In order to go into a gas, it takes heat from whatever is in the box, thus cooling it. The heat created by the motor and the compressor is fanned away by means of cooling fins attached to the bottom of the refrigerator.

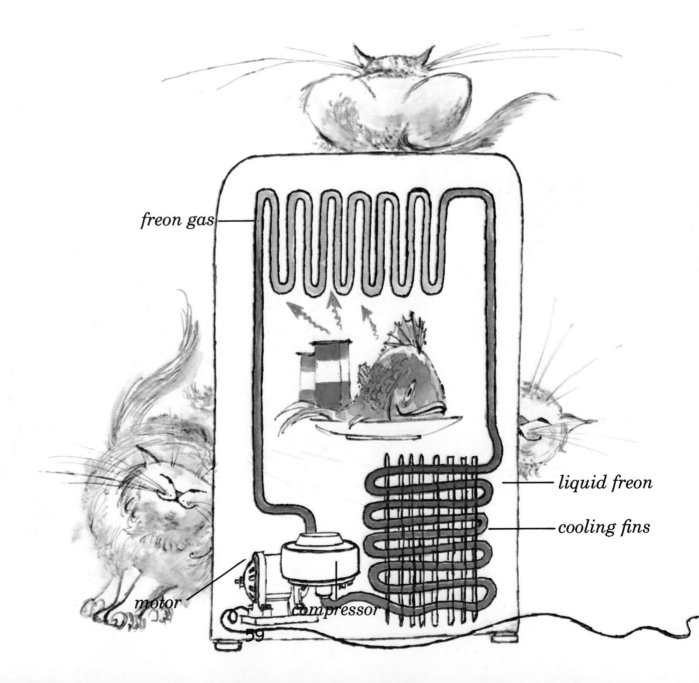

freon gas

liquid freon

cooling fins

motor

compressor

59

The Sewing Machine

Elias Howe

Elias Howe was a machinist in Massachusetts, but he did not make enough money to support his family. His wife used to take in sewing and mending to make a little extra money. One evening, as Howe watched his wife sewing the endless seams late into the night, he decided to invent a machine that would do the same thing.

He made a rough model of a machine that used two threads to make the stitches, instead of one. The stitch was made with a curved needle and a fast shuttle. He finally managed to sell his invention in England.

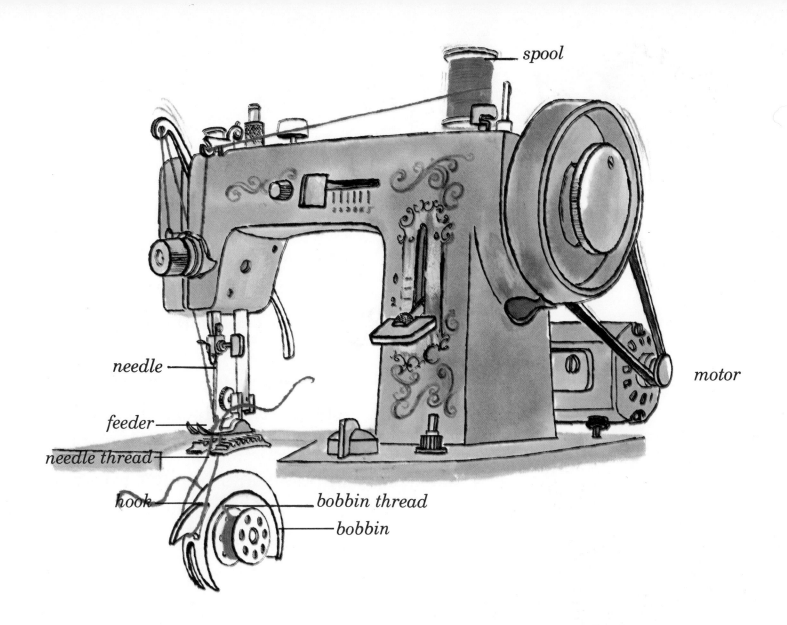

spool

needle

feeder

needle thread

hook

bobbin thread

bobbin

motor

The sewing machine can be run either by a foot pedal or by an electric motor. There are two spools of thread. One on top and one underneath called a bobbin. When the threaded needle goes through the cloth it carries a loop of thread down to the bobbin. When it is at the lowest point, the loop is caught by a hook on the bobbin. As the bobbin moves in a circle, the loop passes around the bobbin thread and catches. It then releases the loop, and the needle tightens the thread making a lockstitch and then moves back up through the cloth, ready to begin a new stitch.

The Television
Vladimir Zworykin

Vladimir Zworykin is an American physicist who has opened up a whole new kind of entertainment to people. He developed something called an iconoscope which is a special electric eye used in a television camera, and he then developed a cathode ray tube which is what makes it possible for the television set to turn electrical impulses into pictures. Having seen what could be done with the radio, Zworykin decided to make something that could send pictures through the air, not just sounds. He succeeded in 1934.

screen · picture tube · electron gun

When the television camera takes pictures, it doesn't use film the way a movie camera does. The light given off by the objects being filmed creates a pattern of electrical impulses on a special screen inside the camera. These impulses are then picked up by an electron gun which scans them from left to right and sends them off in a regular wave pattern. The television set turns these impulses back into sound and pictures. The set also has an electron gun which sprays the impulses it has just received onto the television screen. The light-sensitive chemical on the screen glows when it is hit by the electrons and forms a picture.

The Cotton Gin
Eli Whitney

Young Eli Whitney was always very good at mending everything in his father's workshop. Once when he was a boy, he even took apart one of his father's watches and put it back together again so well that no one ever knew it had been opened. In 1793, he was visiting a friend in the South, and some cotton planters asked him if he would make a machine that could take the seeds out of cotton. At that time, one person could clean the seeds out of 50 pounds of cotton in a day. Eli's machine, watched over by one person, can clean one thousand pounds of cotton a day.

The principle of the cotton gin is really quite simple. It sifts the cotton through wires strung too close together for the seeds to pass through. A sawtooth roller pulls the cotton along so that it passes through the wires. The seeds all drop out, and then another roller with brushes takes the cotton off the saw teeth.

Whitney's gin was worked by hand with a crank, but soon it was attached to a motor which turned the crank even faster. Now, the part of harvesting cotton that was the hardest, and the most time-consuming, has been made simple by machine.

motor

brushes

sawtooth roller

wires

The Vacuum Cleaner
Ives W. McGaffey and John Thurman

One of the problems with sweeping things up with a broom is that something always manages to escape from the dustpan. In 1869, Ives McGaffey invented a special kind of cleaner that could suck up dust. McGaffey's sweeper was operated by hand, though. Finally, John Thurman figured out a way to attach a motor to the sweeper. This powered the fan inside. Even though regular old-fashioned brooms are still used, almost everybody has a vacuum cleaner because vacuum cleaners get up every last bit of dirt and dust.

The End

A vacuum cleaner sucks up whatever is on the floor and blows it into a bag. The front of a vacuum cleaner has a brush roller which sweeps the dirt and dust off the floor or rug. Behind the brush roller is a fan. When the fan is on, it creates a partial vacuum. That means that there is less air around the fan, so air from the area right around it rushes in to take its place. This sucks up the dirt and then blows it into the bag. The bag has tiny, tiny holes in it so that the air can blow through, but the holes are too small for the dust to blow through, so it collects in the bag. When the bag is filled, it can be emptied out and then more sweeping—or vacuuming—can be done.

dust bag

fan

motor

brush roller